William Washpot

BUMBLEBEE PAPERBACK EDITION

A CIP catalogue record for this title is
available from the British Library.

ISBN: 978-1-83934-050-5

Bumblebee Books is an imprint of
Olympia Publishers.

First Published in 2022

Bumblebee Books
Tallis House
2 Tallis Street
London
EC4Y 0AB

Printed in Great Britain

www.olympiapublishers.com

Mrs Washpot

William Washpot

Bumblebee Books
London

HOW TO TRAIN
YOUR

CHAPTER ONE

Nobody knew William wanted a dog. Nobody, not even his mum. So what was his surprise when he received a mysterious invitation!

William Washpot
is invited to the
'Get one Free'
dogs' home.
No.11 Acacia Avenue.

It was signed Mrs Gercher.

Get One Free
Dogs Home

He stuffed the invitation into his pocket and on his way home from school he rang the bell of the 'Get One Free' dog's home.

Instantly the air filled with the sound of barking dogs. William rang the bell again.

Get One Free
Dogs Home

"ALRIGHT! ALRIGHT! I CAN HEAR YOU!" came the sharp response and a little old lady poked her head round the door. "WHAT DO YOU WANT?" she snapped.

William showed her the invitation. "HOLD IT UP BOY!" she said.

William held it up and as he did a withered hand shot out and yanked him in.

"I AIN'T GOT NO PUPS!"

"I don't want a pup," said William.

He hadn't told his mum yet. He knew she would go nuts if he took a pup home.

The hall was full of dogs, some had short legs, some had long legs. Some were black and some were not, but they were all barking and jumping up at William.

"Do you have any quieter ones?" he said.

They went into a room full of dogs lolling around on armchairs watching television.

"Too sleepy!" said William

"WELL THAT'S THE LOT! COME BACK NEXT WEEK THEY'RE ALWAYS DUMPING DOGS!"

She shuffled back into the hall.

It was then that William noticed something in the corner by the door. It was a box.

What's in there?" he said.

"Oh him! You can't have him, he's gonna be put down." In the box was an old dog, his fur matted and covered in mud, his tail gave a feeble flick.

"I want this one!" said William, pleased that he had found the dog he wanted at last.

"You can't 'ave 'im! The vet'll be 'ere soon, he's gonna be put down."

"I'll pay!" said William, feeling in his pocket for his birthday money.

"Well," she said, "if you're gonna pay, but don't bring him back when he drops dead!"

"I won't!" said William and he picked up the box and rushed out. "You're not going to drop dead, are you?"

On the way home he bought a brand-new red leather collar and lead with the money left over.

It was then that William told the GREAT LIE. He told his mum he found the box on a bench in the park.

"Take him into the garden and wash him," said Mrs Washpot. "He's not coming in till he's clean."

It took three buckets of soapy water to wash all the mud off, but when he was done…

"Mum… Mum come and see!"

His fur, it was long and it was shiny.

"I'm going to call him Ginger," said William proudly.

SCHOOL

CHAPTER TWO.

Ginger followed William everywhere. They walked to school together and after school Ginger was there waiting at the gate.

Ginger slept at the foot of Williams bed and in the morning jumped up and down to wake him up.

Then, one cold, grey, winter's morn the old dog didn't wake up. William pulled the covers back in alarm.

"What's up, Ging?" he cried.

Ginger opened his eyes and looked at William. He gave his tail a feeble flick, buried his head in his paws and went straight back to sleep.

William pulled him out of bed, dragged him downstairs and plonked him on his favourite chair.

"What's wrong?" he said.

"He's old," said William's mum.

That day William was late for school.

“WHERE HAVE YOU BEEN BOY?” said his teacher.

William wanted to tell him about Ginger. He wanted to tell everyone… he tried, but he could not speak.

After school he rushed to the gate.

There was a group of boys looking at something in the gutter.

It was Ginger

William bent down and picked him up and took him home.

“I’m sorry,” said his mum.

William could not cry, he could not speak, he just sat there with Ginger till his dad came in.

They dug a hole in the garden in the shade of the apple tree where Ginger liked to rest.

They buried him properly with a cross of sticks.

On top they lay flowers.

"He hasn't spoken since Ginger died!" Mrs Washpot told the doctor. "It's been ten days!"

The doctor looked down William's throat. "There's nothing wrong with him," he said. "Get him another dog, he'll soon forget Ginger."

But William did not want another dog. He wanted Ginger.

That night William dreamt that Ginger was jumping up and down on his bed.

CHAPTER THREE.

But it wasn't Ginger, it was an elf!

The elf knew all about William and how sad he was that Ginger had died.

He had come to cheer him up.

"Would you like a barley sugar?" he said, reaching into one of his pockets.

And William spoke for the first time. "I-I don't like barley sugars."

"That's a pity," said the elf. "If you liked barley sugars you'd be as happy as I am." And he popped one in his mouth and chucked the wrapper on the floor.

William could smell soot on him, could feel his bony elbow as he rummaged through his pockets.

"You'll like this!" And he flung his hand into the air and the air became filled with snow.

It snowed and snowed and snowed until William's bedroom was covered in snow.

It snowed on his bed and in his hair.

The elf made a snowball and chucked it at William. William made one and chucked it at the elf. They made a snowman.

Then, for no reason at all, the elf took a snowflake from the air and put it in his pocket and the snow disappeared.

"Awesome!" said William

Then from a tiny pocket in his coat the elf took a bottle. He took out the stopper and dripped a drop of goo onto Williams brand-new carpet!

The goo grew and grew into a great green gooey puddle.

"Come on!" said the elf jumping in.

"You've got to like puddles, everyone likes puddles."

William looked on in horror as barley sugar wrappers bobbed up and down and a dried-up apple core floated out from under his bed.

"Don't you be worrying about what your mother will say!" And he took a tin whistle and started playing the merriest of tunes.

William's feet twitched uncontrollably, and he rolled up his pyjamas and jumped in.

They jumped and splashed and did not stop until they heard footsteps on the stairs.

"My mum!"

The elf froze! He did not want to meet William's mum! He dived under the covers. William was quick to follow. The door opened, William held his breath. "It's midnight," said his mum. "I'll make you a nice cup of hot chocolate!" And she left the room, closing the door behind her.

"Did I hear 'hot chocolate'?" said the elf scrambling from the covers. "I love hot chocolate!"

William looked at the carpet, there was not a trace of puddle, sweet wrappers, or apple core. "It's your coat, its magic, isn't it?" His coat, it was red with gold buttons There were pockets on it. Pockets down it and up it. There were pockets on pockets and pockets around it.

"This old thing!" The elf smoothed the rough cloth. "Everyone's got one where I come from, it's where we keep our things. Time I introduced me self. Me names Yor!"

William shook his sticky, outstretched hand and Yor told him how long ago, he and the other elves had lived in the forest. How men had come and chopped down the trees and how the elves had run to the only safe place they could find, the disused chimney stack in William's house.

"But isn't it dark and smelly up there!"

"Yes," said Yor, "we love it dark and smelly."

"Do you think you might like a coat? A coat of your own to keep your things in. What do you think?"

William nodded his head excitedly.

"We will have to make a list of everything you want." And he took a note pad and pen from his pocket. "What would you be liking?"

William did not have to think long.

"I would like a puddle."

Yor wrote 'pudol'. William was sitting right next to him. He saw him write it. He wrote slowly and carefully, but he spelt puddle wrongly. William knew this because he was very good at spelling.

"And snow." Then William asked for a tin whistle just like the one the elf had played and Yor wrote 'tin wisol.'

Yor then took out an old tin hat, fixed it most firmly on his head, tied it under his chin, lifted a flap, pressed a button, and instantly disappeared. Then instantly re-appeared.

William was amazed. "Awesome," he said.

"Would you like an invisibility hat?" asked Yor

William nodded.

"I need to measure your head," said Yor and he took out a tape measure.

"It must fit perfectly, and you must be sure to tie it tightly under your chin. If you lose it when you are invisible you will be invisible forever."

Yor wrote down William's head measurements.

"It has to be polished every day without fail, or it will not work," said Yor.

"I can do that!" said William, promising himself that he would keep it always tied firmly under his chin! "What's next?" he said.

William screwed his neck to see what other stuff the elf had, trying to get some ideas. Then in one of the pockets, the one nearest to Yor's heart, William saw a mountain and flying in the clear blue sky, a tiny dragon.

Yor lifted her out. Slowly she grew and rose before them breathing fire. She shook her head and preened her scales.

"Come with me," said Yor climbing onto her back.

The window opened and as the cold wintry air filled the room the beast spread its wings and they flew out into the night.

"My mum!" called William.

"Don't you be worrying about your mum," said Yor. "Time stands still when you're flying on the back of a dragon."

They flew out over the town, looking down on the streets and houses where the elves forest once stood, William gripping tightly to the tails of Yor's coat.

When they returned the elf ran his hand over the dragon's back and by the time he reached her scaly tail she had become so small he could lift her back into his pocket.

"That was cool," said William, "I would love a dragon."

"Every day she has to have five vegetables," said Yor. "They have to be steamed."

"No problem," said William.

Yor wrote 'dracon'.

"How many pleasures is that?" said William.

Yor looked at the list. "Five," he said.

William wondered if that would be enough. He could think of no more,

"Yes," said Yor, "five is enough. You can add more whenever you want."

William liked that idea.

"Is that all?" said Yor.

William thought about Ginger, he thought about asking for another dog, but he didn't want another dog, he wanted Ginger.

"What I would really, really like is an iPad pro!" he said.

Yor looked cross. He put his pen and book firmly back in his pocket.

"We don't have iPads," he said, "they interfere with our magic."

William was disappointed but when he thought of all the other stuff he had, he didn't really mind.

"Come on then," said Yor, "we must go."

William looked puzzled. The little old man jumped from the bed and made his way to the chimney.

“Where... where are we going?” said William.

“To get you a coat.”

“But where?”

“Up the chimney.”

“But, I’m too big.”

“Hold my hand.”

William took Yor’s hand and they became as small as mice as they stepped into the hearth.

From above the sound of chains jangled as a platform descended. They climbed on, side by side, and began to ascend, their legs dangling into the void below.

CHAPTER FOUR.

Beams of light shone out from windows up in the chimney.

Yor and William stopped at the first window. Seated around a table, were four elves.

"They're making toys for Father Christmas to give the children," explained Yor.

William wondered about Father Christmas.

"Yes," said Yor, "Father Christmas visits us. We have Christmas just as you do."

"But how does Father Christmas get into the chimney?" asked William.

"He has the power, just as you have, when he touches the chimney pot, he becomes small enough to enter."

"Have you spoken to him?"

Yor nodded. "When he comes to pick up the presents, he stops for a cup of tea and a chat."

No one noticed William and Yor

They moved further upwards. Through the next window cobbler elves were busy mending shoes and tinker elves repairing pots and pans.

Through the next window, seated at a table, were a family of elves eating pancakes. They waved excitedly when they saw William and Yor.

"It's breakfast time," explained Yor.

"But it's the middle of the night!"

"We wake up when you're asleep and we go to sleep when you're awake."

The next window looked onto a room with tables and chairs neatly lined up in neat rows. On the wall was a large blackboard.

"The school room." Explained Yor.

Next to the window was a door.

"This is the door to the garden. At night we climb onto the roof, shin down the drainpipe and away to forage for food."

They were now at the very top of the stack, the platform swayed and stopped. “That’s it. We’re here.”

William’s feet sank deep into the crisp black soot. They were now in a tunnel. There were two lanterns, Yor gave one to William.

“I have to leave you now.” He spoke softly in a whisper as if afraid to be heard. He handed William the list he had made in the bedroom below. “Give this to Ramekin, he is expecting you.”

He then gave William this warning. “Speak to no one but Ramekin.”

Then he turned and walked away.

William called after him, "Where shall I go?"

"Follow your nose," came the reply, "follow your nose."

William held the lantern high. In front of him was a long dark tunnel.

He turned back looking for Yor, but Yor was gone.

He began to make his way along the tunnel but hadn't gone far when a sudden draft caught the lantern. It flickered and died leaving him alone in the dark.

"Yor," he called.

"Yor," the words echoed back to him

"Yor," he called again. "Yor!" But there was no answer. William wanted to go home. He thought of his mum in the kitchen below making his hot chocolate. He wished he had never met Yor. He sank to his knees in despair.

CHAPTER FIVE.

Then, from the corner of his eye, he saw a flickering light, getting nearer and nearer. Someone was coming.

"Yor!" he called. "Yor!" But it was not Yor, it was another elf. He drew close.

"You here for a coat?" he said, holding his lantern close to William's' face. His voice was rough and ill humoured. "I bet Yor sent you." He lowered the lantern and started to pace up and down. "Yor is a fool, always so happy, always laughing and joking. Life is such fun for Yor. Pompous upstart! Just because he is the eldest, he thinks he knows everything. I bet he told you we haven't any iPads. Well he's a liar." The elf half laughed, half screamed. "Of course, we have iPads! We have the very best." And he shoved an iPad right under William's nose. "He never told you about this, did he? Let me have your list, it won't take long to cross off all this rubbish, you can have an iPad instead."

William was just about to say that he didn't want an iPad when a door opened filling the tunnel with light, and a voice penetrated the silence.

"Who's there?"

"Ah! You must be William, I'm Ramekin I've been expecting you. Come in, come in,"

He ushered William into a room lit by the glow from a fire blazing in the hearth. "Sit down, sit down," said Ramekin.

He took William's lantern and pointed to a chair beside the fire. Then he asked to see William's list. William passed it over. Ramekin was silent for a long time. William held his breath.

"Well young man," he said at last, "it's not a long list. However, it's a list of such pleasures as to befit a most honourable young man. Your pleasures are granted," he said, "and so long as there are no mishaps, a coat of pockets will soon be yours."

"Nothing will happen, sir," said William, "I shall be very careful."

Ramekin lit William's lantern and opened a door. "Follow the stairs until you come to the inner sanctum," He said, "you will be told what to do when you get there."

CHAPTER SIX.

William lifted the lantern high and began to climb, a door slid open. Icy cold air spilled over him as he found himself in a chimney pot, a chimney pot amphitheater, and he was standing centre stage.

Every seat was taken. Row upon row filled with the little people who lived up the chimney.

An elf came in carrying a pedestal. It was placed at the front of the stage.

William stepped out onto it. Someone entered with a coat carefully folded across his arms.

It was Yor.

He came onto the stage right next to William and helped him with his coat. It felt warm and comfortable, and William was filled with overwhelming joy. His heart leapt and a smile lit his face. He was no longer worried but was full of hope and excitement.

Slowly it became silent, as snow began to fall.

Yor plucked a flake from the air and William put it in one of his pockets.

Then came the goo.

All the while Yor was at William's side telling him what to do. William looked up into the heavens. Silhouetted against the sky, its wings outstretched, was the dragon.

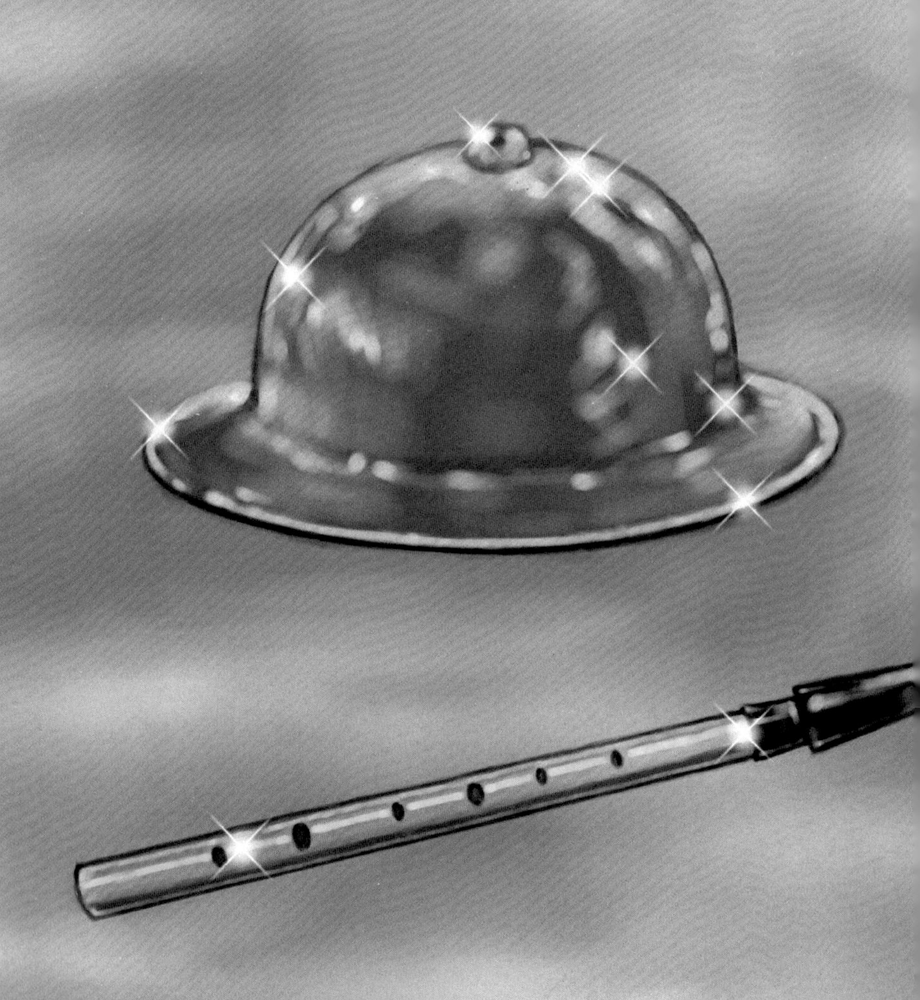

Then the invisibility hat glistening in the light from the moon.

Then the whistle came floating through the air.

William's pockets were filled, and he could not wait to return home.

But the elf he had met in the tunnel, came rushing onto the stage. In his hands was the iPad.

"Here," he called, "take it. It's yours, take it before it's too late."

As William reached out there was a great roar from the crowd.

They rose from their seats and lunged at William tearing at his coat.

The pedestal wobbled. William toppled. He tumbled, twisting and turning down the chimneystack.

The last he remembered was landing with a thump on his bedroom carpet.

CHAPTER SEVEN.

When he opened his eyes, his mother was standing over him in her hand the hot chocolate.

"What happened?" He moaned. "Where's my coat?"

"What coat?" she laughed, pleased that William could talk. "You must have been dreaming."

"It wasn't a dream, it was real, they gave me a coat and a dragon."

"Sometimes dreams can seem so real that you think they are really happening," said his mum.

CHAPTER EIGHT.

The very next day a box arrived for William.

"A strange old lady delivered it," said Mrs Washpot. Inside was a pup. His tail, it was long it was curly. His fur, golden. "She said that he's the son of Ginger."

"I shall call him Goldie," smiled William.

William thought that he had dreamed about Yor and the iPad man and all the elves living up the chimney. Then one day his mother called him, she had been cleaning his bedroom.

"William?" she said. "I didn't know you liked barley sugars."

"I don't," he said.

But he knew someone who did.

He went straight to his room and looked up chimney and there grinning down at him was Yor.

Epilogue

For many years Yor and his companions continued to live in William's chimney.

Mrs Washpot started growing potatoes and vegetables in the garden.

And William did finally get his coat of many pockets!

He even spoke to Father Christmas.